Sam and the Show Steers Save Christmas

A BOOK BY
Shannon Scofield

ILLUSTRATED BY
Sergio Drumond

Sam loves Christmas.

It's his favorite time of the year.

As a matter of fact, there is only one thing he loves as much as Christmas, and that is…

…his show steers!

When you think about it, Christmas and show steers seem like a funny pair.

But not to Sam!

Because he and his show steers actually saved Christmas one year.

What, you don't believe me?

I know it may sound strange, but let me explain.

Sam always wondered, he wondered, and wondered and wondered some more.

He wondered how Santa was able to deliver toys to children all over the world in just one night.

How was that even possible?

So he asked his mom.

8

"*Mom, how will Santa deliver toys to ALL the kids in the world, ALL by himself, before tomorrow morning?*" asked Sam.

"*Well my love, Santa has many helpers, and a lot of Christmas magic up his sleeve*", she said smiling.

"*Now get to bed, because Santa doesn't arrive until you are sound asleep.*"

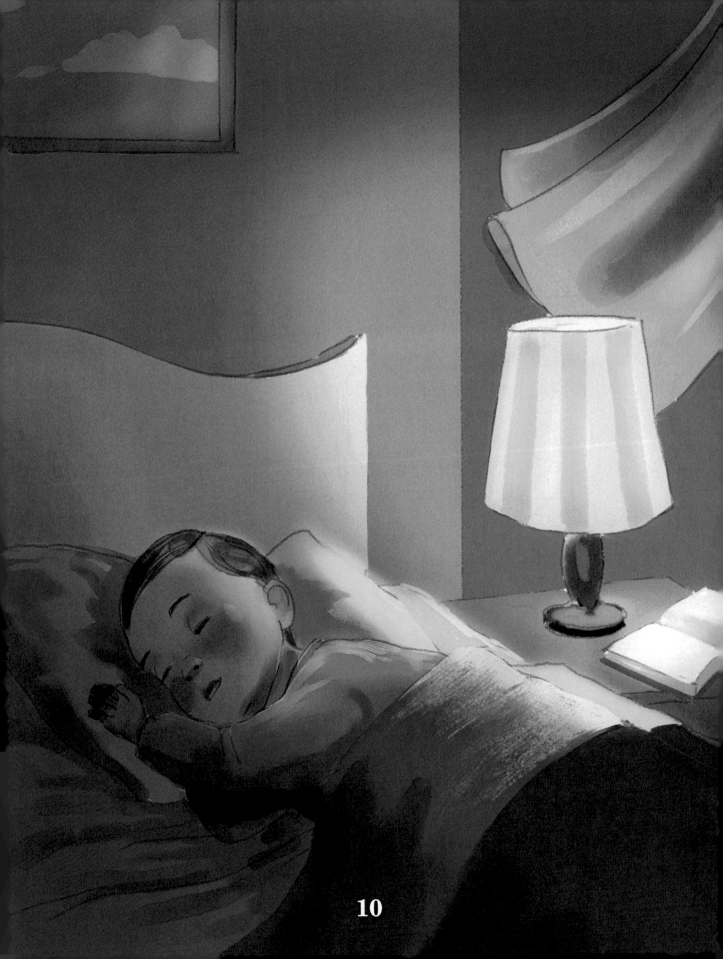

Sam crawled into bed, snuggled under his cozy blankets and yawned.

He fell asleep thinking all about Santa.

Zzzzzzzzzzz...zzzzzzzzzzzz... zzzzzzzzzzz...

Crash! Bang! Boom!

Sam startled awake.

"*What was that?*"
he wondered, hearing a loud ruckus
coming from the roof.

He jumped out of bed, ran downstairs,
pulled on his boots and bolted outside.

When he got to the front porch, Sam looked up. Waaaaaaay up!

He blinked, rubbed his eyes and blinked again.

Sam couldn't believe what he saw.

Could it really be?

Because right there, on top of his roof, was Santa, two elves, one sleigh and eight very sick looking reindeer!

Sam saw Santa pacing back and forth, so he called up to him.

"Hey Santa, what's wrong?"

"It's not good, Sam!"
said Santa, looking worried.

"The reindeer have eaten too many treats along our stops tonight and they are too sick to fly. We may have to postpone Christmas."

"WHAT?!?!" shrieked Sam.

"You can't postpone Christmas, there will be so many sad kids!"

"I know Sam, I hate to disappoint all of the children, but I really can't think of any other way."

Just then, Sam looked over at the corral and had a big idea.

"Santa, we could bed down the reindeer in our barn for the night and you could use my show steers to pull your sleigh."

Sam ran to the barn and came back
pushing a bale elevator.

He propped it against the roof
and one by one the elves sent the
reindeer sliding down, followed by
Santa and the sleigh.

Together, Sam and the elves tied the reindeer into the show bed, making sure that they were comfortable.

When he was finished, Sam raced over to the corral to introduce Santa to his show steers.

There were eight in total, each with a glorious and thick coat of shiny, fluffy hair that Sam had worked hard to clip and groom.

The steers stared at Santa in his fancy red suit, looking a little confused.

"*Santa?*" asked Sam.

"*How will you get my steers to fly?*"

With a twinkle in his eye, Santa reached into his pocket and pulled out a little velvet pouch filled with sparkly dust.

Santa picked up a pail of grain and
dumped it into the feed trough
in the pen.

Then, grabbing a handful of dust, he
sprinkled it on top of the grain.

Sam's show steers gobbled it all up.

Once they were done eating, Sam
hitched his steers to the sleigh.

The elves borrowed his blower and
fogged one last sprinkle of dust over
the entire string until they sparkled
and shimmered.

They were ready to go, and not a
moment too soon.

Santa winked at Sam and with a snap of his wrists, they were off.

Sam watched as the show string began to pick up speed.

Suddenly, their feet lifted off the ground and it was as if they were running through mid-air.

Sam waved and yawned as they disappeared into the night sky.

He was very tired and decided to get some sleep before his show string returned.

There would be work to do come dawn.

In the morning, Sam stretched in his bed then jolted awake remembering his adventure the night before.

Racing into the barn, he found eight very tired show steers enjoying the Christmas hay he had left for them.

Sam smiled to himself, so happy that he was able to help Santa.

But he was also a little bit sad.

How would anyone believe what had happened?

42

As Sam walked into the house, feeling a little glum, something caught his eye.

It was a special package under the Christmas tree with his name on it.

He picked it up and read the tag:

"Dear Sam, thank you for lending me your show string. They did a fine job leading my sleigh. Christmas wouldn't have happened without you! Love, Santa".

Sam ripped open the package and found a shiny silver and gold belt buckle engraved with a picture of his show steers pulling the sleigh and the words

"Santa's Grand Champion Helper".

And that, my friends, is how
Sam and the show steers
saved Christmas!

Made in the USA
San Bernardino, CA
23 October 2016